Tangerine and Kiwi

Visit the Cheese Maker

To Jacques, Bernard, François, and Juliette,
my first readers, my loves

– Laïla

© 2005 Bayard Canada Books Inc.

Editor: Mary Beth Leatherdale
Content Editor: Katherine Dearlove
Designer: Stephanie Olive

Publisher: Jennifer Canham
Production Manager: Lesley Zimic

English translation copyright © Sarah Cummins from *Mandarine et Kiwi: La fondue au fromage* published by Éditions Banjo in 2004.

Special thanks to Jean-François Bouchard, Paule Brière, Susan Sinclair, and Professor Art Hill, Department of Food Science, University of Guelph.

We gratefully acknowledge the financial support of the government of Canada through the Book Publishing Industry Development Program (BPIDP), the Canada Council for the Arts, and the government of Quebec (SODEC) for our publishing activities.

Library and Archives Canada Cataloguing in Publication

Héloua, Laïla
[Mandarine et Kiwi. English]
        Tangerine and Kiwi: Visit the cheese maker / Laïla Héloua; illustrator, Nathalie Lapierre; translator, Sarah Cummins.

Translation of: Mandarine et Kiwi.
ISBN 2-89579-070-1

        I. Lapierre, Nathalie II. Cummins, Sarah III. Title. IV. Title: Mandarine et Kiwi. English.

PS8615.E46M3613 2005   jC843'.6
C2005-903972-8

Printed in Canada

Owlkids
49 Front Street East, Suite 200
Toronto, Ontario M5E 1B3
Ph: 416-340-2700
Fax: 416-340-9769

From the publisher of

chirp chickaDEE OWL

Visit us online!
www.owlkids.com

Tangerine and Kiwi

Visit the Cheese Maker

Story: Laïla Héloua
Illustrations: Nathalie Lapierre

Translation: Sarah Cummins

Hello. My name is Tangerine, and this is my brother Kiwi. Here are my mom and dad.

Today Dad is cooking up a yummy new recipe, cheese fondue. It's a gooey, cheesy mixture. We use forks with long handles to dip vegetables and bread into the tasty treat.

A few days ago we went to buy fresh cheese for the fondue from Jersey's dairy farm.

← Us at Jersey's Farm

When we got to the farm, we saw cows grazing beside a fence. There must have been hundreds of them, and they were all so big! Kiwi was a bit afraid of them.

Dad scooped Kiwi onto his back so he wouldn't
be scared. Kiwi petted at least four cows!

Mr. Jersey pulled out a stool and a big bucket to show us how he milks the cows. He even let us try!

Then we went into the cheese factory to see how Mr. and Mrs. Jersey make cheese. The factory smelled like stinky feet! Kiwi played hide-and-seek behind the door, but he couldn't hide from the smell.

Everyone has to wear a funny cap
in the cheese factory. The caps
keep stray hairs from falling
into the cheese.

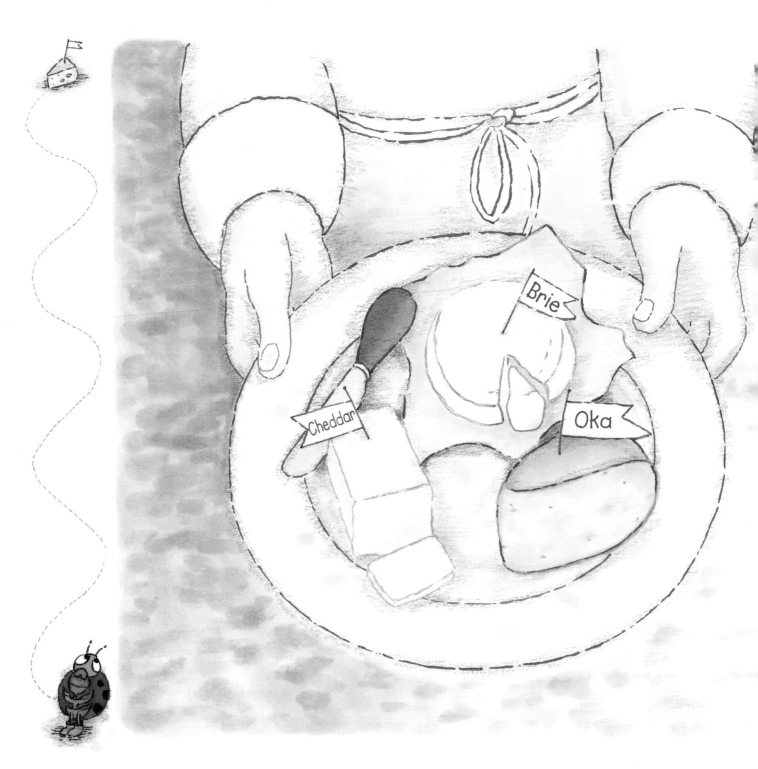

Mr. and Mrs. Jersey make many different
kinds of cheese. Kiwi and I tasted a bunch.
Some were creamy and some were spicy,
but they were all so good!

Mr. Jersey gave Dad his favourite recipe
for cheese fondue. Dad can't wait to try it!
We helped Mom and Dad pick cheese
for the recipe.

As we were getting ready to leave, a big
delivery truck chugged to a stop in the
driveway. It came to take the Jerseys'
cheese to the market.

Then Kiwi and I waved goodbye to the cows. Kiwi wasn't afraid of them anymore.

How Cheese is Made

1 The cheese maker starts with **milk**. He adds an ingredient called an enzyme to separate the milk into solid chunks, called **curds**, and a liquid, called **whey**.

2 The cheese maker **stirs** the curds and whey until they become smaller and firmer. Then he drains off the liquid.

3 Then, the cheese maker **presses** the cheese curds into big, **round** moulds.

4 The cheese maker **soaks** the cheese in brine, which is very salty water. It gives the cheese **flavour**.

5 The **cheese** sits on shelves for weeks or months to let the flavour grow stronger. Then it's **ready for eating**!

"Time to eat, kids!"

"Hooray! I'm so hungry!"

With an adult's help, try Mr. Jersey's **favourite fondue.**

Mr. Jersey's Recipe for Cheese Fondue

250 g (8 oz.) Emmenthal cheese
250 g (8 oz.) raclette cheese
250 g (8 oz.) Gruyère cheese
1 clove of garlic
125 mL (½ cup) dry white wine*
pepper, to taste
1 pinch grated nutmeg
1 loaf French bread, cut in cubes
1 large platter of lightly blanched vegetables (cauliflower and broccoli florets, zucchini rounds) and raw vegetables (cherry tomatoes, mushrooms)

1. Cut the cheese into small pieces.
2. Peel the garlic clove and rub it all over the inside of a fondue pot. Then pour in the wine.*
3. Place the pot over low heat. Add the cheeses and stir constantly until the cheese is melted. Or melt the cheese in the microwave, stirring often. Add the pepper and the nutmeg.
4. Put the fondue burner in the middle of the table and place the pot over it, keeping the flame low so the fondue will stay creamy.
5. Each person spears a piece of bread or vegetable on the end of a long fondue fork and dips it into the fondue.

* Instead of wine, substitute chicken broth with a couple teaspoons of lemon juice. Or use non-alcoholic wine.